Jack and the Snackstalk

1 Moldylocks and the Three Beards

2 Little Red Quacking Hood

Read more of Princess Pink's adventures!

3 The Three Little Pugs

4 Jack and the Snackstalk

Princess Pink
AND THE LAND OF
FAKE-BELIEVE

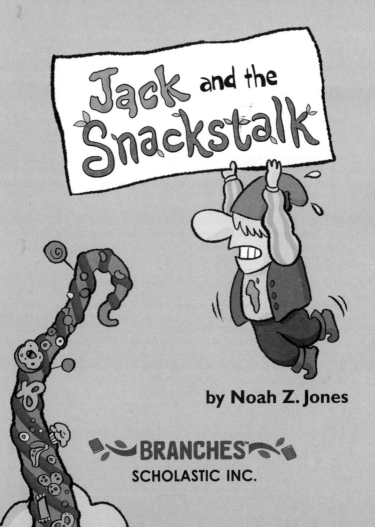

Jack and the Snackstalk

by Noah Z. Jones

BRANCHES
SCHOLASTIC INC.

To my dynamite editor, Katie Carella,
who has been instrumental in bringing
the Land of Fake-Believe to life.

Copyright © 2016 by Noah Z. Jones

All rights reserved. Published by Scholastic Inc., *Publishers since 1920.* SCHOLASTIC, BRANCHES, and associated logos are trademarks and/or registered trademarks of Scholastic Inc.

The publisher does not have any control over and does not assume any responsibility for author or third-party websites or their content.

No part of this work may be reproduced, stored in a retrieval system, or transmitted in any form or by any means, electronic, mechanical, photocopying, recording, or otherwise, without written permission of the publisher. For information regarding permission, write to Scholastic Inc., Attention: Permissions Department, 557 Broadway, New York, NY 10012.

Jones, Noah (Noah Z.), author.
Jack and the snackstalk / by Noah Z. Jones.
pages cm. — (Princess Pink and the Land of Fake-Believe ; 4)
Summary: It is scary movie night at Moldylocks' house; the guests are Princess Pink, and Moldy's cousin Jack, who has brought some nasty-tasting jelly beans for a snack—but when the beans sprout into a pillar of snacks the three friends climb up and find themselves sharing a tasty but dangerous adventure in Snackland.
ISBN 0-545-84861-X (pbk. : alk. paper) — ISBN 0-545-84862-8 (hardcover : alk. paper) — ISBN 0-545-84863-6 (ebook) — ISBN 0-545-84864-4 (eba ebook) 1. Fairy tales. 2. Jellybeans—Juvenile fiction. 3. Snack foods—Juvenile fiction. 4. Humorous stories. [1. Fairy tales. 2. Jellybeans—Fiction. 3. Snack foods—Fiction. 4. Humorous stories.]
I. Title. II. Series: Jones, Noah (Noah Z.) Princess Pink and the Land of Fake-Believe ; 4.
PZ8.J539Jac 2016
[Fic]—dc23
                                                    2015011354

ISBN 978-0-545-84862-6 (hardcover) / ISBN 978-0-545-84861-9 (paperback)
10 9 8 7 6 5 4 3 2 1   16 17 18 19 20

Printed in China   38
First edition, January 2016
Edited by Katie Carella
Book design by Will Denton

◆ TABLE OF CONTENTS ◆

This is Princess Pink. Her first name is <u>Princess</u>. Her last name is <u>Pink</u>.

Princess does not like princesses, fairies, or ballerinas. And she REALLY does not like the color pink.

Princess <u>does</u> like skateboarding and doing karate. And she REALLY likes drawing cartoons.

Princess searched high and low for snacks. She found broccoli buns, coleslaw squares, and wacky wheat germ balls.

What are we going to eat?

I'm sure Moldylocks will have good snacks.

Princess placed her magic magnet on the fridge. Then she turned it to the left. A blast of light filled the room. The fridge stopped its usual <u>**HUMMmmm**</u> sound. It began to sparkle and shine.

Princess opened the door. The gross snacks were all gone. Now the door led to the Land of Fake-Believe. A butcher, a baker, and a candlestick maker were rowing a boat across the sky.

Land of Fake-Believe, here we come!

Princess stepped inside her fridge.

Then she climbed down the ladder.

A big shadow fell on Princess just as her feet touched the ground. Reggie covered his eyes.

· CHAPTER TWO ·
Wacky Wereworms

Two huge wereworms closed in on Princess.

The wereworms took off their heads.
Moldylocks and her cousin Jack were
inside the costumes.

Moldylocks had brought a third giant wereworm costume for Princess.

You can be a wereworm, too!

This costume is crazy-cakes!

Yes, it is!

Then Princess asked Moldylocks and Jack a <u>very</u> important question.

Jack proudly held up a half-gallon tub of cream cheese.

Princess knew what they needed. They needed candy.

Does Fake-Believe have a candy store?

Of course! Come on!

· CHAPTER THREE ·
Magic Beans

On the way to the candy store, the four friends bumped into Mother Moose.

Mother Moose walked with them for a while. But then he smelled cream cheese. Mother Moose stopped in his tracks.

Mother Moose pulled Jack to the side. He offered to make a trade.

Mother Moose made the trade. Then he ran home to make some bagels.

23

Jack caught up with the girls to tell them about his amazing trade.

Guess what! Mother Moose traded me for the cream cheese!

Hooray! What did you get?

I bet it's something yummy!

Jack held up the bag of jelly beans.

Mother Moose said these are <u>special</u> jelly beans!

That's all you got? And they're pink?! I can't stand pink!

I'm not even a fan of <u>moldy</u> jelly beans. I never would have made that trade!

The girls were unhappy with Jack for making such a bad trade. Jack was unhappy with the girls for being unhappy. And Reggie was just unhappy. No one wanted to go to the candy store anymore.

Let's just go watch the movies.

It's about time.

Okay. My house is right around the corner.

SIGH

SIGH

SIGH

SIGH

Moldylocks led Princess, Jack, and Reggie into a swamp.

Welcome to my house!
Don't worry, nobody bites.

Moldylocks even showed Princess the kitchen.

Scaredy-Pants Wolf helped me pick out the oven.

I'd love one of Scaredy-Pants's yummy pies right now!

I invited him. But he was too scared to come. He doesn't like wereworms.

It was almost movie time! The friends sat down on the couch. All at once their tummies grumbled.

Princess, Moldylocks, and Jack each took a small handful of jelly beans.

Princess, Moldylocks, and Jack spit out the jelly beans.

They tried as hard as they could to get rid of the awful taste.

Princess and Moldylocks gulped down the Dragon Fire juice. But it didn't help.

Princess grabbed the rest of the jelly beans. She tossed them out the window.

Moldylocks turned off the lights and Jack pushed PLAY. The friends were so excited to watch wereworm movies that they didn't see the ground outside begin to glow.

· CHAPTER FIVE ·
Snackstalk Shock!

When the first movie ended, the friends stood up.

As soon as the three friends walked outside, they got a real SHOCK! A gigantic snackstalk was growing next to the tree house. And it led all the way up to the clouds!

Jack took a bite of the snackstalk.

Moldylocks and Princess stopped him before he could eat anymore.

The three friends started climbing the stalk. Princess led the way.

41

The friends climbed up and up . . .

and up and up . . .

AND UP!

At long last, they broke through the clouds. They couldn't believe their eyes—or their stomachs.

The friends stood in a very strange and wonderful land. <u>Everything</u> was made of tasty snacks.

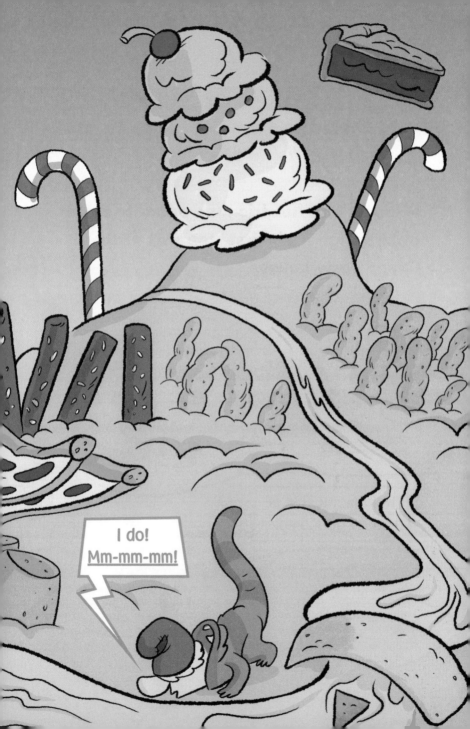

◆ CHAPTER SIX ◆
Fee-Fi-Nacho-Cheese!

Princess and her friends wanted to taste everything! Their first stop was at the Great Tasty Lakes.

Next, they played baseball in the Royal Cheese-Doodle Gardens.

Finally, they had a sword battle on the Great Wall of Chicken Fingers.

Then, Jack spotted a huge castle. A golden glow poured out of one of its windows.

Look! I bet the best snack EVER is in that room!

Maybe. But if it's locked up in a giant castle . . .

. . . Something or someone must be guarding it!

Jack didn't wait for the girls. He raced to the castle.

Jack paused at the castle's enormous doorway. But then he ran inside.

The girls tiptoed into the castle.
Everything was huge.

Someone <u>really</u> big
must live here.

I just <u>really</u> hope
no one is home.

All of a sudden, there was a rumbling sound. The ground started to shake. Jack ran into the hallway.

Run! We have to hide!

What is that? An earthquake?

I think something—or someone—BIG is coming!

A loud voice rang through the castle.

FEE-FI-NACHO-CHEESE!
I SMELL THE BREATH OF SNACK THIEVES!
BE THEY BIG OR BE THEY SMALL,
I'LL MASH THEM INTO MINI MEATBALLS!

·CHAPTER SEVEN·
Golden Egg Roll

Princess and her friends found a hiding spot upstairs. They hid just as a VERY big bunny stomped into the room.

There was no way the friends could get past the big bunny without being seen. They needed a plan.

Maybe we'd run faster without our costumes?

Wait a minute! That's it!

What's it?

Our <u>costumes</u>! We'll pretend we're REAL wereworms! We'll fool Big Bunny!

I hope this works! Jack—come on!

The three friends fell to the floor. They wriggled and squirmed past Big Bunny. . . right out the front door!

Princess, Moldylocks, and Jack raced across Snackland. They stuffed snacks into their costumes as they ran.

They slid down the stalk lickety-split and landed with a thud. Tasty treats spilled out of their costumes.

The friends went back inside the moldy tree house. They dumped their snacks on the table.

Check out all of our snacks!

That place had the best treats!

Great! Can we start the next movie now?

Moldylocks turned off the lights and pushed PLAY.

After the second movie, the friends stood up for another stretch. They had already eaten all of the snacks.

We need more snacks.

We could go back up. Right, Princess?

I guess so. It should be easy-peasy in our costumes.

I'll wait here.

Princess, Moldylocks, and Jack climbed back up the snackstalk.

•CHAPTER EIGHT•
Wereworm Wiggle

The friends quickly filled their costumes with tasty treats. But Jack kept looking toward the castle.

Don't even think about it, Jack. There are plenty of treats right here.

But none are as tasty as the Golden Egg Roll!

Jack ran to the castle. Princess and Moldylocks chased after him.

They all rushed inside.

Big Bunny was not happy. She was stomping around the castle. And she was yelling. The friends dropped to the floor and started wriggling.

FEE-FI-NACHO-CHEESE!
I SMELL THE BREATH OF SNACK THIEVES!
BE THEY YOUNG OR BE THEY OLD,
I'LL SMUSH THEM INTO A JELL-O MOLD!

I hope our trick works a second time!

It will!

Shh!

Big Bunny spotted the three wriggling wereworms! She scooped them up and dropped them onto a giant plate.

YUM! WEREWORMS ARE MY FAVORITE TREAT!

Wait! Can I taste the Golden Egg Roll before you eat us?

JACK?!

Big Bunny poured ranch dressing over the friends. Princess had to think fast.

Big Bunny picked up Princess.

Princess held her breath as Big Bunny leaned in close. Then she bonked Big Bunny on her big bunny nose.

Big Bunny grabbed her sore nose with both hands. The plate—and the three friends—tumbled to the ground.

Luckily, a giant stack of pancakes broke their fall.

Jack grabbed the Golden Egg Roll! The friends ran like crazy. The ground shook as Big Bunny chased after them.

Jack kicked the Golden Egg Roll over the edge of the clouds. The friends all leapt onto the snackstalk. Suddenly, the stalk began to rock back and forth.

With a loud snap, the stalk broke. Moldylocks whistled for help as they all fell down, down, down . . .

CHAPTER NINE

So Long, Snackland!

Tunacorn swooped in and rescued them!

Thanks, Tunacorn!

I'm so glad you heard my whistle!

Where's my Golden Egg Roll?

With Tunacorn's help, Princess and her friends safely put their feet on the ground. But three dark and spooky shadows fell on them.

The friends wriggled and squirmed away from the <u>real</u> wereworms. Tunacorn tiptoed after them.

Just then, Jack saw something glowing in the bushes.

The Golden Egg Roll!

The Golden Egg Roll had broken open in the fall. Bright sparkly bits were all over the place! The friends ate and ate.

Then it was time for Princess to leave.

Reggie was sound asleep on the couch.

Looks like we missed the third movie.

That's okay! We just LIVED a wereworm movie!

Princess hugged Moldylocks and Jack good-bye. Then she scooped up Reggie. Tunacorn flew them to the door that led out of Fake-Believe.

Thanks for the ride!

Princess stepped through her fridge.

Noah Z. Jones

is an author, illustrator, and animator who creates all sorts of zany characters. He hopes that kids who read this book learn about the danger of eating too many snacks. He also hopes they learn how to avoid being eaten by fifty-foot-tall women named "Bunny." Noah has illustrated many books for children, including *Always in Trouble*, *Not Norman*, and *Those Shoes*. Princess Pink and the Land of Fake-Believe is the first children's book series that Noah has both written and illustrated.

How well do you know THE LAND OF FAKE-BELIEVE?

Reread pages 12-13. How does Princess react to seeing wereworms? Is her reaction surprising? Why or why not?

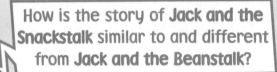

How is the story of **Jack and the Snackstalk** similar to and different from **Jack and the Beanstalk**?

What do Princess and Moldylocks think about Jack's trade with Mother Moose? Explain.

Do **you** think the friends should have gone back to the castle for more snacks? Write a letter to them. Explain what you think they should have done and why.

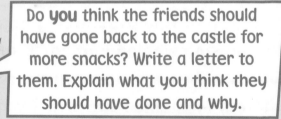

Use words and pictures to describe the snacks **you** would like to see at the top of the snackstalk.